MAX

The Stubborn Little Wolf

MAX
The Stubborn Little Wolf

ISBN 0-439-31789-4

12 11 10 9 8 7 6 5 4 3 2 1   2 3 4 5 6 7/0

Printed in the U.S.A.   24

First Scholastic printing, February 2002
Typography by Matt Adamec

MAX

The Stubborn Little Wolf

MARIE-ODILE JUDES

illustrated by
MARTINE BOURRE

translated by Joan Robins

SCHOLASTIC INC.
New York Toronto London Auckland Sydney
Mexico City New Delhi Hong Kong Buenos Aires

uick as a wink, when anyone asked Max
what he'd like to be one day,
the little wolf always said: "I want to be a florist."

That answer made Papa Wolf so angry that his tail twitched.
Finally he laid down the law. "Wolf fathers and sons are hunters,
have always been hunters, and always will be hunters.
You, my son, will follow the family tradition. And that is that!"

"But I don't *like* hunting," said Max.

"That's impossible," roared the big wolf.
"All wolves love to hunt!

"After all," Papa Wolf added in a sweeter voice, "there's nothing more enjoyable than chasing a really plump little pig, capturing him, and then cooking him in a big pot with onions and apples."

"I don't like meat!" said Max.

Papa Wolf laughed at that. "It seems to me you really liked that leg of lamb on Sunday. You ate five slices!"

"I like meat that you buy, but not meat that you hunt," explained the little wolf. "I won't be a hunter. I will have a beautiful flower shop. With the money I earn selling tulips, roses, and daisies, I'll be able to buy all the meat I can eat. I want to be a florist, and that is that!"

The stubbornness of his son
kept Papa Wolf awake all night.
While Max slept peacefully,
the big wolf paced up and down the kitchen.
"I must stop my son from becoming a florist,"
he muttered over and over again.
"If I don't, I'll lose my mind."

The next evening, in the middle of dinner,
Papa Wolf suddenly had an idea:
*HO-HO-HO! I know how to stop Max from becoming
a florist. He just has to learn to love hunting.
That'll make him forget about those good-for-nothing flowers!*

The big wolf banged his paw on the table to be sure
Max was paying attention. "Tomorrow," he declared,
"we will go hunting for rabbits and young boars.
And if I don't manage to make you a hunter, my son,
I'll eat my hat, I will!"

At dawn the next morning,
Papa Wolf shook Max awake.
"Get up quickly," he ordered.
"We're going hunting!"

Papa Wolf made Max drink hot tea
with pepper to wake him up,
and hummed a hunting song.

When they arrived in the forest, the big wolf whispered,

"SSHH, we'll hide here.

As soon as a rabbit passes by, we'll jump on it

and put it in the basket."

A few minutes later,

a rabbit pushing a wheelbarrow appeared.

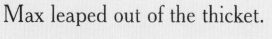

Max leaped out of the thicket.

"Quick! Save yourself, little rabbit," he shouted.

"My papa wants to eat you!"

The rabbit dropped his wheelbarrow
and ran off without waiting to hear more.

"What's the matter with you?" yelled Papa Wolf.
"Why did you do that?"

"Because I don't like hunting," said the little wolf.
"I already told you that.
Hunting is nasty, cruel, horrible.
I will never be a hunter. I . . ."

Max stopped speaking
and stared with big round eyes at his papa.
The big wolf was eating his hat.

In the middle of the night,
another idea popped into Papa Wolf's head.
HO-HO-HO, he said to himself.
This time I know how to keep Max
from becoming a florist.
I'll just tell him that it's a dangerous job.
If that doesn't change his mind,
I'll eat my pillow, I will, I WILL!!

At breakfast the next morning the big wolf said, "It's fine to be a florist, my *little* son, but do you know that it is dangerous work?"

"Weally?" mumbled Max, his mouth full of crispy flakes.

"Yes, indeed," said Papa Wolf. "You might prick yourself on a rose thorn, or slip and fall in the mud, or cut yourself with the garden shears . . ."

Max jumped up and kissed his father.

"Don't worry, my *little* papa," he said.

"I'll be very careful.

I'll put on gloves so I don't prick myself,

boots so I don't slip in the mud, and . . ."

Max stopped speaking
and stared with big round eyes at his papa.
The big wolf was eating a pillow!

The next afternoon,

Papa Wolf woke up from his snooze with a sneeze.

"HO-HO-HO!" he cried out. "Now I really know

how to keep my son from becoming a florist.

I'll make him hate the smell of flowers!"

The big wolf jumped into his car

and went to a big department store.

He bought three bottles of strong-smelling perfumes:

rose, lilac, and violet.

That very night he crept into Max's room
and emptied the three bottles of perfume
all over the blanket, the pillow, and
the head of the little wolf.

The smell was so strong that
it made even Papa Wolf
feel sick.

"If this doesn't make Max hate flowers,"
the big wolf whispered, "I'll eat Grandmother's dishes,
I will, I will, I WILL!!!"

As soon as Max got up the next morning,
he went to find his father.
Papa Wolf was shaving in the bathroom.
"There's a very strange scent in my room,"
Max said. "It smells like roses and lilacs and violets.

"Papa," the little wolf said, taking a deep breath.
"I have something to tell you.
I no longer want to be a florist!"

Papa Wolf was so shaken by this news
that he cut himself with his razor.
"Is that really true?" he asked,
trembling with joy.

"Yes, it's true," said Max,
as Papa Wolf sat down in his favorite chair.
"I want to make perfumes instead! I think
what I *really* like about flowers is their smell."

The little wolf stopped speaking and
stared with big round eyes . . .

"Papa?"